Teddy's Toy Trouble™

Written by Jean Waricha
Illustrated by Diana Magnuson

MARVEL BOOKS

Teddy Bear lived with his mother and father in a tiny den. One Saturday morning while having breakfast, Mrs. Bear asked Teddy, "Did you straighten up your room yesterday?"

"Yes," replied Teddy as he poured some raisins into his cereal.

Later that day, Mr. and Mrs. Bear peeked inside
Teddy's tiny room, and they almost fainted.
What a mess it was!

"Teddy, dear," instructed his mother firmly, "your room is too tiny for all your toys. You don't even play with some of them anymore. Please give some away . . . or throw them away."

Teddy sadly looked around his messy room.
How could he part with his old airplane or his very
first pull-toy?

How could he give away his red wagon? He had just painted it.

His rock collection was probably worth millions—if and when he found the right buyer.

Teddy lovingly looked at his baseball trophies and equipment. Last year his Little League team won second place.

And never, never could he throw out Two-Ton, his favorite elephant. Two-Ton protected him from the monster that lived under the bed.

Teddy sat on his chair and looked again at his messy little room. "Maybe my friends can help me decide what to do," he said to himself.

That afternoon Teddy and his friends met in their clubhouse.

"This is a common problem," said Mugsy the raccoon. "My mother made me clean my room last week."

"Me too," said Ralph the rabbit.

"Come on, Teddy," said Paula the porcupine. "We know just what to do."

Teddy and his friends got right to work. Then they called for Teddy's parents to come have a look.

"Oh, Teddy," said Mrs. Bear with a big smile on her face. "This is a wonderful sight. Cookies and milk for everyone!"

While Teddy and his friends enjoyed their snack, Mr. Bear noticed Teddy's jacket on the floor.
He picked it up and took it to Teddy's closet.

"Oh, dear!" said Mr. Bear. "This is not the kind of clean-up we had in mind."

Soon Teddy and his friends were back in his room, figuring out what to do next.

They kept busy for a long, long time.

By the time Teddy's friends left, everything was in its place.

That evening after dinner, Mr. Bear said, "Well, Teddy, is your room clean now?"

"Oh, yes," said Teddy. "Come look."

"Now this is more like it," said Mr. Bear. "Would you like me to read you a bedtime story?"

"I'll get my dinosaur book," said Teddy.

Mr. Bear sat down on Teddy's chair. "Umm," he said, wiggling and squirming. "Something is not right. This chair feels lumpy and bumpy."

Teddy watched while his father picked up the seat
cushion and discovered Teddy's rock collection.

"I just can't part with them," said Teddy sheepishly.

"We'll have to figure out what to do with these rocks," said Mr. Bear. "But now let's read."

Mr. Bear reached for the lamp switch, but the lamp rolled away.

"Something is not right!" Mr. Bear yelled, grabbing for the lamp.

"I just can't give my wagon away," said Teddy. "It's always been one of my favorite things."

"Oh, dear," said Mr. Bear. "We'll have to figure out what to do with this wagon."

But just as Mr. Bear was about to sit down again . . . kerplunk! Teddy's old airplane and pull-toy hit him on the head!

"Oh, no!" said Teddy. "Are you all right, Dad?"

"I'll be fine," answered Mr. Bear, rubbing his head.

"I just can't give them up," said Teddy. "We tried to tape them to the ceiling, but they didn't stick."

"There's always a way to fix something that's not right," said Mr. Bear. "Come with me."

Teddy and Mr. Bear sawed and hammered and nailed and painted.

"We're just about done," said Teddy, clapping his paws.

Soon all of Teddy's toys were put away. Well, all but Two-Ton the elephant. Where monsters are concerned, it's best not to take chances.